# BEASTS

# BEASTS



INGVILD
BJERKELAND

TRANSLATED BY ROSIE HEDGER

LQ
LEVINE QUERIDO
MONTCLAIR | AMSTERDAM | HOBOKEN

This is an Em Querido book
Published by Levine Querido

LQ
LEVINE QUERIDO

www.levinequerido.com · info@levinequerido.com

Levine Querido is distributed by Chronicle Books, LLC

Originally published in Norway in 2023 as *Udyr* by Cappelen Damm.


Library of Congress Control Number: 2024942576
ISBN 978-1-64614-513-3

Printed and bound in China

FSC
www.fsc.org
MIX
Paper | Supporting responsible forestry
FSC™ C144853

Published in April 2025
First Printing

This translation has been published with the financial support of NORLA, Norwegian Literature Abroad.

NORLA
Norwegian
Literature Abroad

# ONE.

**The crows gathered around the body like a black eider-**down.

I held my sister, Alva, by the hand.

"What's *that*?" she asked. Her voice was shaking, but she took a step closer.

The crows took flight as one, the flock shrieking hoarsely as they disappeared over the forest.

"Just a deer. Nothing to worry about."

Alva covered her mouth with both hands. Her eyes were wide.

"I don't like it here," she whispered from behind her fingers.

I knelt down beside the deer and rested my palm on its body. My hand turned red with blood.

"Yuck!" Alva exclaimed.

"Not so loud. Alva, you need to whisper," I said quietly, wiping my hand on my trousers. It was already black and grubby. A little blood wouldn't make any difference.

"Come on."

We carried on through the forest.

The trees towered high above us, their sagging crowns bowing and whispering softly. The forest floor was covered in pine needles that absorbed our footsteps. Only the birds shattered the silence, their shrill cries reverberating through the air.

Then the forest opened up ahead of us and we found ourselves atop a crag. There we stood, completely exposed, the white moonlight beaming down on us like a spotlight.

"Oh! Look, look!" Alva cried, pointing at the sea. "A boat!"

"Stop shouting!" I hissed, pulling her down to a crouch to better conceal us.

I peered out at the black, foamy sea and caught sight of the enormous cargo ship gliding by, way out on the water. Too far off to see us.

To save us.

I kept pulling Alva along beside me, but her footsteps were heavy.

"I'm tired," she grumbled, "and my tummy hurts."

All we'd eaten the past few days were a pack of oat cookies and some blueberries we'd stumbled across in the forest. I was tired too, and my stomach ached with hunger.

"We can't stop now," I sighed. "Djupevik is a long way off, and there was that deer . . ."

But no, I couldn't tell her that the deer's body had still been warm, that it hadn't been long since the animal was killed. We were in danger; we had to keep moving.

"But I'm hungry!" Alva said, her bottom lip beginning to tremble. "I want something to eat."

"Here," I answered, passing her the bottle of water. We'd filled it up in a stream we passed earlier that day. The water tasted mossy, but it filled our stomachs. Alva took a large swig and made a face as she swallowed.

"Come on," I said, squeezing her hand. "Just a little further, OK? We'll stop for a rest soon."

"Poor deer," Alva said after a little while. "What killed it?"

"Deer are killed by other animals all the time," I replied, "wolves and bears and things like that. It's normal."

"But there aren't any wolves and bears round here," she objected. "You said! When I was scared! You said!"

"A fox, then. It was probably a fox."

Alva nodded and smiled. A fox. She wasn't afraid of foxes.

She trusted me. Her big brother, who was always so brave and calm.

Her big brother, who lied.

Foxes don't leave two deep, precise rows of bite marks in their prey. Not like the ones I'd seen on the deer's stomach. The ones I'd hidden with my hand, so Alva wouldn't catch sight of them.

The only creatures to leave marks like that were the beasts.

# TWO.

**Someone was coming!**

All of a sudden I heard the snapping of twigs nearby.

Branches were thrust to one side, then swung back, as someone forced their way through the forest.

Fast feet bolted through the surrounding woodland.

They were heading straight for us.

We ran.

Pushed our way through a tangle of dry branches and bushes that whipped our faces. Into a bog, giving no thought to where we were stepping. We were quickly soaked but continued onward, our socks and shoes slurping and gurgling, up onto a hill covered in heather, past a few more prickly bushes, over a rocky knoll, and down yet another hill. I tripped over a stone and dragged Alva down with me as I fell. We tumbled together, rolling downhill, heather and twigs in our faces and mouths—but there was no time to lie there, no time to figure out if we'd hurt ourselves. Even Alva knew that. We were back up on our feet without a moment's hesitation.

We had to keep running, as fast as we could, as far as we could.

But eventually we could run no further. Fear alone can only propel a body so far. A body needs food and rest.

We were tired; so very, very tired.

Alva was so small.

"We need to hide," I whispered.

We found a rocky slope, covered in moss and thick brambles. I squeezed myself backward in between two large rocks, carefully pulling Alva in after me. The brambles were like tangled barbed wire; they snagged our clothing and scratched our bare skin. The space between the rocks was so narrow I could hardly breathe. Alva sat on top of me and I could feel her pulse throbbing like the pendulum of an old clock.

Something stepped out into the clearing. It stood there, just across the bog.

Alva whimpered softly and I placed a hand over her mouth, the other over my own.

The fear was like an enormous black bird within me. It beat its wings in panic. But still I made no sound.

We heard it moving through the bog. Gurgling sighs from the holes each step left.

We heard wheezing from an open jaw filled with long, sharp teeth.

It came closer and closer.

Stopped just by the rocky slope.

In the moonlight I could see the beast's legs between the stones and brambles. They were long and covered in sleek black fur. Its hooves were hidden in the grass. Hanging by its sides were two long arms with slender hands, and thick claws that curled inward, in the shape of a spiral.

When they get angry, their claws unfurl, transforming into long, razor-sharp swords.

I'd seen it with my own eyes when they killed Mom.

# THREE.

**Alva's body trembled against my own.**

Fear flapped its black wings within me.

We didn't make a single sound.

I thought about the last time I'd seen Mom.

"Take Alva and run," she'd said, then, the blood seeping out beneath her body as if she were lying on a red rug.

I did as she'd told me. I took Alva, nothing else, and I ran.

Maybe I should have refused. Or returned later, to see if Mom was still there on the grass in front of our house, clutching the big kitchen knife.

But now I had Alva to think about. What would happen to her if I went back, if the beasts were still there, if I didn't survive? Who would take care of her then?

Things weren't like they used to be.

We waited on the rocky slope.

The beast waited not far away.

It glanced all around. Pricked up its ears.

We held our breath.

Waited.

Finally, the furry legs moved.

We heard the sound of hooves on stone, branches snapping as it made its way into the forest, heading north.

We stayed where we were for a while. I was breathing fast, and the air surged through my chest, as if I'd just been sprinting.

"We need to take a different route," I finally said, coaxing us out from between the rocks and the brambles. "We need to take a detour."

"But why?" Alva's hands were still clasping the fabric of my sweater, her knuckles white. "I don't want to take a detour."

"Because it went the way we're supposed to be going," I answered. "We can't exactly follow it, what if it turns around?"

"What if it's waiting for us in Djupevik?" Alva said.

I hadn't thought of that.

I couldn't think of it.

I didn't have an answer.

"It's not," I said, no more, no less. "Come on!"

We clambered to the top of the rocky slope, taking it one boulder at a time. I had to drag Alva along after me on some. We scraped our hands and knees as we went.

From the highest point we could see in all directions, and though the moon lit up the bogs and crags, I didn't dare look for the beast. We got down on our hands and knees and crawled over the peak and down the other side, heading east, away from the sea.

The sky changed color as time passed. The dark blue turned gray, then light blue. The sun slowly worked its way up over the horizon and the rays stretched out across the grassy fields before us.

There were no rocks or trees here, nothing to hide behind.

"If we hear anything, we'll lie down on our tummies and hide in the grass, OK?" I said.

"Or run away?" Alva suggested.

"They can run much faster than we can."

"OK," she replied gravely.

Someone had set up an electric fence around a field to keep the sheep in, but there was no longer any electricity. There were no sheep left, either. Any livestock had long since been killed and eaten. There hadn't been any food in the shops for a month.

People had started stockpiling all sorts, even in the early days. As soon as the initial shock had passed after the first attack; as soon as they realized the authorities had no control over the situation. People cleared the shops of toilet paper and chocolate, flour and yeast, canned foods and pasta. Eventually there was nothing left but packets of gelatin and nylon stockings and spray starch on the shelves. There was nobody to stock the supermarkets or drive semis over mountains and borders; there were no longer any ships in the harbor. One of the last news reports we'd heard on the radio before Mom had died and we'd fled had been about attacks on farms. These attacks weren't been carried out by beasts, though.

I helped Alva over the fence.

"Ouch! It shocked me!" Alva said, grabbing her tummy. "It hurts! My tummy hurts!"

"There's no power, it's harmless. Stop messing around!"

"OK," Alva answered meekly, then promptly threw up all over the grass. Her vomit was mostly liquid and yellowish green.

"Being electrocuted doesn't cause you to throw up, anyway," I said irritably, tugging at her arm. "Come on!"

"But it hurts! It really hurts!"

"Do you want to wait around here to be killed like Mom?"

"No," she replied tearfully, shaking her head.

"Then come *on*!"

"I think I could eat a whole sheep if I found one," Alva said after we'd crossed the field and a deserted road. "But I'd take the wool off first."

"You'd have to kill it."

"I know. But I'm so hungry I'd do it. I could eat *anything* now. Even *broccoli*." She pondered her words for a moment before adding: "Not sushi, though!"

I smiled. "I don't think there's any sushi out there for you to worry about. Not here, anyway. You'd have to go abroad for that kind of thing."

"Is that where we're going?" Alva asked, stopping in her tracks. "Is the boat in Djupevik going abroad?"

I nodded.

"To the Shetland Islands. We'll go on to Fair Isle from there. I don't think it's far."

"Well, I still don't want to eat any sushi," she said firmly.

"That's fine."

"But I *do* want to go to Daddy."

"He's waiting there for us, I promise."

I took her hand.

Alva clutched her stomach as she walked, and tiny, crystal-clear pearls of sweat glistened on her forehead. She didn't voice any more objections; instead, she just talked about food, what she liked and didn't like, what she missed the most, what she'd eat when we reached Dad.

"Quiet for a second," I said.

"Is there a beast coming?" she asked, sounding timid.

"No, I just . . ."

I placed a hand on her forehead. It was hot and clammy.

"Are you cold?" I asked her.

"Freezing," she replied with a nod, then she threw up once more.

# FOUR.

**I missed grown-ups.**

Mom, Dad, my teacher, the mailman. Literally anyone.

If only someone, somewhere could tell me what to do. How to take care of a sick little sister on the run. No food or clean water or medicine, no bed to tuck her into, no safe place to hide.

All I wanted was to sit down and cry. I wanted to slam my bedroom door and yell at the top of my lungs about how the world wasn't fair, I wanted to play my PlayStation until Mom knocked gingerly, wondering if I'd had time to cool off, if I felt like joining them for a little something to eat. I wanted to sit at the kitchen table with Alva and have a peanut butter sandwich while Mom read aloud to her from a book she liked and Dad clattered plates and cutlery as he unloaded the dishwasher, and Alva would berate him, telling him it was time for *reading,* not for making a racket, that was the rule! And Dad would laugh. *Yes, boss!* he'd say, closing the dishwasher and kissing the top of Alva's head before Mom carried on reading and we carried on eating. I wanted to be there, in the house, with Mom and Dad changing Alva into her pajamas and making sure she took her multivitamin and brushed her teeth. I wanted them to say good night and tuck us in and hang fresh, clean clothes up to dry, to fill the kitchen cupboard with food and the stove with logs, to close the windows and lock the doors, to keep an eye on things. I wanted to go back to that world. And for a moment, my yearning was so strong that I trembled.

"Abdi?" Alva said, squeezing my hand so tight her nails left an indent in the palm. "What's wrong?"

"We need to find a place we can stay for a while, just until you're feeling better," I sighed. "A house, a hut, anywhere."

"A yellow house?" Alva asked.

"Sure, why not, a yellow house," I replied, a little sarcastically. "Any other color simply wouldn't do."

"Well, that one's yellow," Alva said. "Do you think it might be a different color around the back? Maybe they've painted it red on the other side, is that bad? Is it OK if it's only yellow on one side?"

I stared at her. Was it the fever that was making her act so strangely? How sick *was* she?

"Come on," I said. "I'll carry you on my back for a while. Then we'll see if we can find a yellow house, or anywhere else we can stop for a while. OK?"

I crouched down and let her climb up onto my back.

"Let's try the yellow house first," Alva said firmly.

That was when I spotted it too. There, on the hillside, nestled between the trees, a yellow house that seemed to beckon us. *Come on over.*

I was drenched in sweat by the time we reached it. Alva was heavy on my back, her hands like hooks digging into my shoulders.

The house was old, but it had been well maintained. There were flowers growing in the bed along one wall, and on the front steps was a pair of big black boots. I carried Alva around to the back. There was a garage at the far end of the driveway with a wheelbarrow leaning against the wall. A row of apple trees was growing along the fence. Most of the apples were small and green, but a few had turned red. I shimmied Alva down from my back and picked two of them, passing her the larger of the pair. Alva shook her head.

"You need to eat something," I said.

"My tummy hurts."

"Rest for a while, then."

I pulled off my jacket; it was green and baggy and almost completely covered Alva when I laid it over her. She had collapsed in a sleepy heap. My plan was to investigate the garden and house. There might be people here; someone could be watching us through the dark windowpanes, hiding behind a curtain. I smiled and waved, just in case.

A small patch of earth had been dug up in the garden, and row upon row of plants appeared to be emerging from it. Potatoes, maybe? I didn't know anything about growing plants and vegetables. We'd only ever had flowers in our garden at home, and Mom would have to buy new plants from the garden center every year because she could never coax them back from the brink after they started to wilt and die. There were three raised beds next to the patch of earth. One was filled with large pale green leaves. I tore off a leaf and stuffed it into my mouth. It crunched between my teeth, fresh and crispy. Lettuce. In the bed beside the lettuce were carrots. I pulled up two and stuffed them, still covered in sticky brown soil, into my pockets.

I glanced back at the house. Someone had to be living here. Surely nobody would leave a place like this with a garden full of food?

I carried on making my way around the house, back to the driveway in the front. The windows were too high up for me to be able to see inside, but the potted plants on the windowsill were brown and withered. The boots on the step were filled with leaves and dust and dirt; they hadn't been worn in a good long while. I leaned in close to the glass pane in the door and peered inside. It was dark. No movement to be seen. Even so, it was a risk. I took a deep breath and knocked.

"Hello?" I called. "*Hello?* Is anyone home?"

Nobody replied. I listened long and hard for footsteps on the floor. Voices. Eventually I took hold of the door handle, moving cautiously. It was locked.

"Hello?" I shouted again, knocking on the door. "Could you open up, please! My sister is sick. We're all by ourselves. We're not going to hurt you!"

So stupid!

What an idiot I was, standing out here and broadcasting the fact that we were alone and unwell. Hadn't the past few months taught me anything?

"But if you hurt us then we'll kill you! I'm just saying! I'm armed too!" I shouted, peering through the windowpane.

It was just as dark and silent within the house as it had been before.

I made my way back down the steps, stamping my feet threateningly.

On my way over to the garage, I glanced into the garden to check on Alva. She was motionless beneath my green jacket. Fear welled up suddenly, but I forced it back down.

I managed to lift the garage door just high enough that I could crawl inside. It was empty, but on the floor I could make out some tire tracks, and by the wall I found an empty plastic fuel can. Whoever had been living here had owned a car and driven it away. You would only ever leave a place like this if you knew about somewhere better. Safer.

# FIVE.

**Two weeks after the initial attack, the neighbors assem-**bled in our kitchen for a meeting. It had been Mom's suggestion.

"We need to gather whatever resources we have so we can help each other out," she'd said.

The electricity had been out for four days by that point, which was the second power outage since the attack. Luckily we weren't cold—it was summer, and the days were warm and bright—but we complained about the lack of ability to charge our cellphones, the absence of television or internet. The food in our freezers had started to defrost, and Mom had served up apple cake. The neighbors politely helped themselves to small slices. Hunger hadn't set in yet. There was still enough food and medicine to go around and a belief that the authorities would sort things out before too long.

"I doubt the power outage has anything to do with the attack," one person claimed, and the others nodded in agreement.

"The power will be back on tomorrow, mark my words."

"All I'm saying is if those beasts make their way out here, I'll open fire on every last one of them!" our neighbor Kai called. "Don't you worry about that, folks!" He patted his hip as if he was carrying a gun, then gave each of us a nod. The neighbors nodded back and offered him strained smiles. Kai had been second mate on a large ship before his retirement, and nowadays he spent the majority of his time showing up unannounced on people's doorsteps and dishing out advice nobody asked for.

"I'm sure that won't be necessary," Amar said. His son was in my class at school. "The army and police will have everything under control in no time at all."

"Of course," the others replied in chorus. "Absolutely."

And I breathed a sigh of relief—I remember that.

I'd seen the news about the attack: hazy pictures and shaky cellphone footage. Large creatures entering the railway station in the middle of morning rush hour, or a shopping center, or an office building. Nobody knew who they were or where they'd come from. They were described by one reporter as bears, while another claimed they were terrorists dressed up in animal costumes. One witness claimed that they were aliens, which had prompted laughter from the journalist.

The attack was serious. Tragic. But it was also far away.

The whole thing was a bit surreal.

And the adults weren't scared, so I wasn't either. They ate apple cake and discussed the power outage, then each of them returned to their home.

Two weeks later, the neighbors were back in our kitchen. The power had been out for nineteen days. The supermarket shelves were beginning to look bare. People were staying at home with their doors locked. The beasts had spread; they were moving closer.

I was allowed to attend this meeting, as I had been the first, but Alva had to go to bed. It took Mom a long time to settle her.

"I want Daddy to put me to bed! I'm not going to sleep until Daddy comes home!" she shouted, just as she had every night since we'd last spoken to him. Dad was an ornithologist who'd been away on a work trip to the bird observatory on Fair Isle when everything happened. It was on a little island in the middle of the North Sea.

"I'll be back as soon as I can," he'd told us, the last time we spoke, before Mom's phone battery died. There was still no sign of him.

"I'm not going to sleep until Daddy comes home!" I heard Alva shout again.

Mom looked tired as she closed the bedroom door behind her.

"Finally!" she said, smiling. "Silence!"

I perched on the kitchen counter and Mom stroked my cheek as she leaned over my shoulder to glance out of the window.

"I hope everyone comes tonight," she said. "It's more important than ever that we all stick together."

"I'm sure everyone feels the same way."

"I hope you're right. But selfishness spreads like wildfire."

"What do you mean?"

She didn't say anything back, just stared out at the blue summer evening sky.

They moved into our driveway as a flock, those leading the way wielding flashlights. The late summer evening was bright enough to allow a view of the road, but the flash-light beams swept across the hedges and forest behind in great yellow arcs while Kai stalked the periphery of the group, shotgun in hand.

One by one they filled our kitchen, adult bodies crammed in tight, all of us enveloped in the clammy, sour-smelling odor of unwashed clothes. Several of the men had grown beards since I'd last seen them. They talked among themselves in hushed voices. Kai pushed his way through the room and sat down at the kitchen table. He laid the shotgun across his lap before folding his hands and resting them on the tabletop, clearing his throat loudly. Silence fell almost instantly. Kai smiled contentedly as his gaze moved over all the faces in the room.

"We need supplies," he barked. "It's time we got a group together and headed into the city." The others nodded in agreement.

"We'll need a list, then," somebody at the back of the room chipped in. "There are people here in need of medicine."

Mom found a sheet of paper and a ballpoint pen and passed them to Kai, who immediately handed them over to his pal Bruno.

"Write," he commanded. Bruno nodded and took note of each of the medicines the neighbors called out.

"Make sure to get plenty of dried goods and canned food," one said.

"And candles," said another.

"And matches."

"Batteries."

"Toilet paper."

"And tampons." Kai groaned and rolled his eyes.

"Hardly a necessity, are they?" he said with a snigger. Bruno glanced up from his list, bewildered.

"You're man enough to grab a few boxes of tampons, aren't you, Kai?" Mom grinned, and several of the others laughed. "They won't bite." Kai stared at Mom, incensed. He didn't like being mocked.

"Are we even sure there's any food left in the shops?" another neighbor chimed in. "That it hasn't already gone?"

"We'll get what we need elsewhere, if that's the case," Kai asserted. "We'll be going in armed."

"Why do you need to be armed?" The question slipped out of me before I could think twice.

"We're going to make sure we get what we need and that nobody will be taking it from us," Kai replied, shaking his head in resignation.

"We need to share what we find," Mom said.

"Do you and your kids want food on the table or not? I can certainly take your share if you don't need it. Is that what you want?"

"No," Mom answered. "But there's no need to lose our heads, that's all I'm saying. We're still living in a civilized society, surely. We can't just go round threatening people to get our hands on the things we want."

Things had gone very quiet in the kitchen. None of the neighbors said a word; nobody voiced their agreement with Mom. Kai was the only one looking at her. He gazed long and hard, his eyes cold.

"How would you like to come with us, eh?" Kai asked. "Show us how we can do things *nicely*?"

"Sounds great," Mom said, flashing him a wide smile. "I'll grab the tampons, shall I? Save you from having to touch them?"

Alva woke up as the neighbors were on their way out. They chatted loudly now, their footsteps heavy, and amid the noise and commotion we heard Alva's faint cries and more calls for Daddy.

"I'll go in and see her," I told Mom. She smiled in surprise and mouthed a silent *thank you*.

Kai waited beside Mom, his arms crossed and his entire frame looming over her. It was obvious there was something he wanted to get off his chest. I sent a supportive glance in Mom's direction as I sneaked past them into the bedroom.

It took me a while to get Alva back off to sleep. I was a poor substitute for Dad.

When I eventually made my way back into the kitchen, Mom was sitting at the table with Amar and a young man I didn't recognize. Their voices were low but they were deep in conversation. I hopped up onto the kitchen counter and Mom glanced over at me briefly. I was allowed to stay.

"A sea crossing is our only hope," the young man said.

"Surely it's safer to stay put?"

"My dad has managed to connect with some others via radio," the young man replied. "We've been in contact with people all over, and they're all saying the same thing. We can't go east. There are too many of them that way. And they're spreading out fast. The Swedes have been completely overrun, and we've heard about attacks in Denmark, Germany, and Poland. Before we know it they'll have invaded us here too. If we're going to have any chance of surviving this, we need to go west by sea."

"The army and the government will sort things out eventually. And they'll get help from other countries. It will be OK," Mom insisted. "We just need to stick it out together."

"If we're not killed first," Amar said. "Or at the point of starvation, or dying for lack of medication."

"I don't plan on hanging around, in any case," the young man said. "There are boats leaving from Djupevik and heading out to Shetland and the Faroe Islands. I haven't heard about there being any monsters out there. It has to be safe."

# SIX.

**I picked up a large rock I found behind the garage and** carried it into the garden. Alva was still lying motionless under the apple tree. The sun warmed us, and the forest behind the house was perfectly still. I tried not to think about what might be within.

I threw the stone at the glass pane in the French door and tugged at my sleeve, wrapping it around my hand before reaching through the remaining shards of glass and unlocking the door from the inside. There was a stale, unoccupied smell inside the house, and nobody launched a surprise attack as I passed through the living room and made my way into the largest bedroom with Alva on my back. I laid her down in the double bed and tucked two duvets around her. She whimpered faintly but didn't wake. Her forehead was red hot now.

I thought long and hard about whether to take off my shoes. I hadn't removed them since we'd left Mom on the grass outside our house. My feet were longing for fresh air. But it was much harder to escape without shoes on, if anyone should turn up on the doorstep. These were the things that occupied my mind these days. Escape. Survival. Planning, always planning. The old me, the boy who complained about his homework; who left his bike lying outside the front door when he got back from practice, even though Mom had told him hundreds of times to put it in the garage; the boy who never ate his crusts and who thought that emptying the dishwasher was hard work; he would never have survived this.

I placed my shoes in the middle of the hallway with the laces undone so they'd be easy to slip back on, if anything were to happen. I found a backpack in the hallway closet and stuffed a wool blanket, a large knife, and a flashlight inside.

I crouched by the backpack, and as I closed it, a wave of dizziness washed over me.

The world around me seemed to slide about, like a coloring book where nothing had stayed within the lines. My head suddenly felt so incredibly heavy that I had to lie down. Even with my eyes closed, the world continued spinning. Was I sick, like Alva?

"No," I protested weakly. If I were to fall ill we'd be helpless. I couldn't.

"You're not unwell. Pull yourself together," I whispered.

I took a deep breath, grabbed the rag rug beneath me, and squeezed it tight.

My legs were shaking as I got up, but still they carried me. Using the wall to help support myself, I slowly made my way through the hallway and into the kitchen. I needed something to eat.

On one side of the kitchen was an old black wood-burning stove with a hot plate on top, and lined up along the windowsill were the withered plants I'd spotted from outside. A floral tablecloth lay on the table, and a cup with coffee stains inside it had been left sitting on top of a crossword magazine. Someone had made it halfway through one puzzle, filling the boxes with elegant penciled handwriting. I found a glass in the cupboard and turned on the tap, but it coughed and spluttered drily and not a drop came out. When I opened the fridge, it was like sticking my nose in a box of sour-smelling gloop. I felt a wave of nausea rise within me, but I pulled my sweater up in front of my face, breathed in the overpowering scent of my own unwashed body instead, and worked my way through the food in the fridge. The ketchup looked OK, and the same was true for the pickled gherkins. Eggs had a long shelf life—I'd learned that at school when we'd been studying food waste and the environment. Behind the box of eggs was a large block of cheese. It was moldy on one side, but I could cut that off. In the drawers I found a pack of crackers, some oats, two jars of jam and eight cans, a combination of pasta and meatballs, ham, baked beans, and fruit cocktail. I shoved most of the cans, the pack of crackers, a can opener, and two spoons into the backpack. All of a sudden the tap spluttered two loud, dry coughs and clear water flowed into the sink.

It's strange how happy I felt in that moment. The fear within me had neatly folded back its wings and tucked them in, at rest. I filled the stove with logs and pages I'd torn from the crossword magazine and managed to get the fire going on my first attempt. The yellow flames crackled gently as fried eggs and canned ham sizzled in the frying pan I placed on the stove, and the morsel of cheese I stuffed into my mouth tasted better than anything I'd ever eaten.

A silent peal of laughter seemed to pulse through me: I could do this.

I served the food up on two large plates and carried them into Alva's room. Even deep in the throes of her fever and slumber she could smell the food, and she opened her eyes as I set one of the plates down beside her on the bedside table. I crept into bed beside her.

"Mummy always brings us breakfast in bed when we're sick," Alva said with a smile, tearing off a piece of fried egg. And medicine, I suddenly realized. When we were ill, she'd give us medicine.

"Wait there." I shoved an entire egg into my mouth, then crept back out from under the duvets.

I found an orange box of aspirin in the bathroom cupboard. I filled a large glass to the brim with ice-cold, clear water.

"Here," I said. "Take your medicine, you'll be feeling better in no time."

"Promise?" Alva asked.

I nodded. "Cross my heart," I said.

Once Alva had fallen asleep again, I began to explore the house. Hallway; kitchen; a living room with another wood-burning stove, a bookshelf, and a sofa covered in soft cushions and blankets; two bedrooms and a bathroom. A door in the hallway led to the basement.

I lingered at the top of the steep basement staircase for a moment before I dared to descend. Anything or anyone could be hiding down there. I grabbed the knife from the backpack, placed one hand against the wall, and held the knife in the other hand. The stairs creaked. My heart hammered in my chest.

I found myself in a large, open space. Light flooded in through two high windows. I could smell woodwork and engine oil. Beside the staircase were a washing machine and a tumble dryer with a red laundry basket on top of it, filled with clean, folded bedsheets. Beneath the windows was an old carpenter's bench, and there beside it, a paint-flecked kitchen chair with a jagged heart carved into it saying, *H + O forever.* Hanging from the wall above the bench was a large homemade wooden board with different-size hooks and various tools on them, and below the ceiling were shelves filled with identical, clearly labeled plastic boxes.

The opposite wall was covered in maps. When I looked closer, I could see that someone had drawn on them with different color ballpoint pens and markers. Comments had been scrawled in various spots, and each location had a number next to it. The largest map showed all of Norway and had the most pen marks. Several cities had been circled in red and numbered. At first, I thought this referred to their size, but then it hit me: it was the order in which the cities had been attacked. It matched with what I recalled seeing on the news. The three largest cities first, then the towns closest to them. There were red arrows pointing away from each of the marked locations. To indicate the direction the beasts had moved in? I quickly searched for our hometown, but there were no red arrows. Whoever had been living here must have left a while ago. I found a pencil stub on the board above the carpenter's bench and drew a thick arrow on the map, pressing so hard the pencil point tore straight through the paper. The beasts had reached us in the end.

# SEVEN.

**Mom was picked up in a van by Kai and Bruno the day** after the neighbors' meeting. Alva and I sat on the front steps and waved them off.

"Don't forget the candy!" Alva shouted after the van as it careered away from our house. "Do you think they'll remember?" she asked, turning around to gaze up at me.

"Don't be stupid." I got up and pulled her inside.

I locked the door behind us, just as I'd promised Mom.

The hours passed slowly. The sun moved all the way around the house. Alva was restless and fussy. I let her build a fort in the living room with the furniture and blankets. She shouted and made a mess. We ate crackers and chocolate spread for dinner, and I sent her to bed not long after, lying to her about what time it was.

When she'd gone to bed, I sat on the kitchen counter and gazed out the window, waiting. It grew darker outside, darker in the kitchen too.

Nobody came.

I nodded off on the counter with my head resting on my arm and my legs tucked up under me. My whole body felt stiff and sore when I woke in the middle of the night. Mom still hadn't come home. That was when I started to feel scared.

She didn't get back until first light the following day. I had moved into the entryway by that point and was sitting with my head against the door, crying. I had been crying for so long, there was hardly a drop of liquid left in me. I'd spent hours listening intently for the sound of a van, but Mom arrived back home on foot. All of a sudden, I heard feet on the front steps, and someone grabbed the door handle.

Mom didn't look good. Her skin was dusty and mucky and her hair was stuck to her head. There was blood on her sweater. The sight of her stopped my tears in an instant, and I helped her onto a kitchen chair. She asked me for a glass of water and gulped it down greedily.

"What happened?" I asked.

"Lot of stuff," she replied with a wry smile. It's what I always used to say when she asked me what'd happened at school, or what my friends and I had got up to that day.

"Stop it," I said. "It's not funny."

"*Moooooom!*" she said, smiling again and looking at me.

"Mom!"

"OK, OK," she replied, stroking my cheek tenderly. "Just give me a second. Is Alva sleeping?"

I nodded.

"Could you get me something to eat, please? Anything, I don't mind. I haven't eaten since yesterday." She pulled the bloodstained sweater over her head. The T-shirt she was wearing underneath was dry; I couldn't see any injuries.

I fetched her an apple and buttered two crackers before refilling her glass of water. She ate slowly.

"What happened?" I asked again.

"Madness," she murmured with a sigh. "OK, OK, I'll tell you," she acquiesced as she finished her last cracker. "We picked Amar up on the way out, then headed straight for the city center. And it was tense, I can't deny it. Kai and Bruno were hyping each other up with all their talk of incompetent authorities, how the only people to survive this will be the ones who take control of the situation for themselves. Their typical conspiracy theory nonsense, I don't know," she said, sighing again.

"And you should have seen the supermarket. It was surreal. It was virtually pitch black in there, they just had a few of those battery-powered lamps lying around, and the place was swarming with people, all shoving each other and trying to grab whatever they could. The poor souls working there were doing their best to keep on top of things, but the checkout machines don't work without any electricity, and people don't have any cash left, so lots of people just weren't paying. It was chaos." She shook her head.

"Kai and Bruno had flashlights and shotguns with them in the shop. They claimed it was in case the beasts showed up, but mostly it was to scare people off, I think. To make sure they got whatever it was they wanted. I've heard there have been problems with deliveries and quite a few people out there are stockpiling goods. We managed to get our hands on some food, at any rate, but no medicine. The pharmacy in the shopping center was closed, there was a sign up saying they had nothing left in stock, so we carried on, stopping in two more supermarkets after that. But it was the same story: very little food and too many people. No medicine. We drove to four different pharmacies, but every single one of them was closed. I could feel Amar getting more and more stressed with every attempt. You know his wife, Lin? She has a heart problem. She could die if she doesn't get her prescription. Her doctor's told them there's nothing he can do, his office was cleared of medication too. I understand that Amar is scared, I do, but something in him changed. After we reached the third closed pharmacy, he suggested we break in. I had to explain to them that it wouldn't do any good; there was nothing in there anyway, breaking the windows wouldn't help matters. That was when Kai suggested we go straight to the people with the medication we need."

"Who?"

"I shouldn't be telling you this," Mom said, letting out a heavy exhale. "I feel—not quite right, not quite *here*, if that makes sense. It's been such a long night, and all of this has been swimming around inside my head the whole time. Everything that happened, all the things I should have said or done. I'm sorry. You don't need to be hearing all this."

"I want to," I insisted.

"But Abdi . . ." Mom said tenderly.

"Mom, please."

"They drove to a nursing home," she went on eventually, her voice low. "From Kai's perspective, it was only fair. The people there are old and sick, but Lin is young. She needs the medicine they've got."

"What about Amar?' I asked, alarmed. I knew Amar. He was kind: a normal man with three kids, a friend of my dad. He'd never steal medication from sick, old people. It didn't make any sense.

"He was desperate," Mom said. "And Kai persuaded him that the world isn't what it once was, that the normal rules no longer apply, that kind of thing. I tried to argue against him, of course, but none of them were listening to a word I said at that point. When we reached the nursing home, they marched straight in, all three of them, with shotguns and baseball bats."

"Did they shoot anyone?" I asked, thinking with terror of Mom's bloodstained sweater.

"No, it was just their way of making sure that nobody tried to stop them. But it was awful. The old people were terrified and Kai and the other two ransacked every room, taking whatever medication they found, regardless of what it was, whether it was on their list or not. And I shouted and argued and tried to stand in their way, to no avail. Eventually Kai got so angry with me that he decided to leave me there. The others didn't say a word, they just went along with it."

"And the blood?" I asked, appalled.

"Just a nosebleed," Mom answered, shaking her head gently. "I had to walk all the way home; that's what took me so long. I tried taking a shortcut, but I was tired and clumsy and fell flat on my face. It's not bad, just a bump. Nothing broken.

"The worst part was having to leave the nursing home without being able to help anyone, without being able to fix the damage they'd done," she went on, sounding distressed. "I gave the nurses Kai's and Bruno's and Amar's names, but I've got no idea if the police have time to follow up on that kind of thing these days. And I don't know if the nurses will manage to get hold of any more medication. All of our systems have failed."

That was when Mom started sobbing quietly.

"And I don't have any food either," she said, trying to dry her face with the back of her hand. "Kai won't share with us now. We've got nothing. I'm so sorry!" The tears ran freely.

"We'll be OK," I said, wrapping my arms around her, and at that moment, Alva burst through the door and threw herself into our arms. I don't know how long she'd been standing out in the hallway or what she'd heard.

"I'm sorry," Mom whispered again, stroking Alva's head.

"It's OK," I replied, and Alva echoed my words, "It's OK, Mummy."

"Dad will be back soon," I said. "He'll sort things out."

Mom nodded and looked at me. "Or we'll have to go and find him."

# EIGHT.

**I don't know if Mom actually meant what she said about** planning to go to Dad.

All the same, something was set in motion then. One evening I was woken very late by the sound of the front door closing, and I found a note on the kitchen table telling me not to worry if she was out when I woke up, that she would be back soon. Another evening, I heard voices in the kitchen, but when I sneaked through the hallway to see who it was, Mom stopped me in the doorway and asked me to go back to my bed.

She never had the chance to tell me what was going on. Never had the chance to share her plan with me.

The beasts came to our house the next day. Two of them, tall and covered in fur, with their claws uncoiled and lifted like swords in front of them.

"Take Alva and run," Mom shouted, rushing outside. I did as she told me. I ran for the forest behind our house, dragging Alva along behind me as she wept. But I couldn't stop myself from looking back, watching Mom fall to the ground, blood pouring out. We forced our way through the shrubs and undergrowth until we were on the track leading to our closest neighbor's house. I carried Alva on my back for the final stretch. She cried and cried until she spotted the white house, the van parked in the driveway, the smoke rising from the chimney. She gave a little gasp, slipped down from my back, and ran up the front steps.

Kai opened the door before she could knock.

"What do you two want?" he asked.

"The monsters came!" Alva shouted.

Kai recoiled.

"*Here?*"

"To our house," I said, out of breath, "there were two of them. You need to come and help my mom!"

"Did they follow you here?" Kai asked, backing into his hallway.

I shook my head.

"No, they're with Mom. They're killing her. Please! You said you'd shoot them!"

Kai retreated further into his hallway and grabbed his shotgun, which he'd left leaning against the wall. I breathed a sigh of relief, then just like that he shut the door in our faces.

"They can smell you! Get away from here before they sniff you out!" he shouted from inside.

Alva looked at me in confusion. "Isn't he going to help us?" she asked timidly.

"No," I said, and the rage that rose up within me was unlike anything I'd felt before. It was cold and hard. Not the kind that made me slam doors or caused my voice to break as I fought back tears. Instead, my pulse slowed. My body felt calm, and my thoughts were as clear as lightning.

It was too late. Even if we managed to persuade Kai to come back with us, even if he shot the beasts, it was too late. Mom was dead. And Alva was my responsibility now. I had to look after her; I had to make sure she had whatever she needed to survive. I kicked the door hard.

"Where's our food? The stuff you took from Mom?" I shouted.

"Go away! You're going to bring them here!" Kai shouted.

"We're not going until you give us our food!" I shouted back.

"I don't have any food!" Kai lied, appearing at the window.

The barrel of his gun was pointing right at us.

"Come on," I said to Alva, and pulled her away.

We made our way back through his yard, between the trees, around the back of the garage, and over toward his granary. All the while I peered around us, looking for beasts. If Kai was right about them following our scent, they could be here any minute. We crawled under his granary and hid behind the staircase, and when I saw Kai move away from the window, I quickly climbed up and tried the door. It was locked. That came as no surprise. His granary was probably filled to the brim with food he'd stolen from people at gunpoint. The windows were dark and sealed tight shut, but I didn't think to break them.

"We'll try the barn," I whispered and quickly swept my gaze over the edge of the forest. There was still no sign of them. We crawled along by the granary and further back, behind some bushes and a trailer. A side door led us into the cowshed. Kai didn't have any livestock, so the bays were filled with garden furniture and old tools.

"See if you can find anything to eat," I told Alva, "but don't make a sound!"

She nodded gravely and sneaked into the cowshed. I searched the barn first, but I could only see piles of junk and old bits of timber. All of a sudden Alva was behind me. I jumped; I hadn't heard her approaching. She handed me an unopened packet of oat cookies and half a bottle of cola.

"Brilliant!" I said. "Come on!"

"Where are we going now?" Alva asked. Her voice was shaking.

"Away from here," I replied. "We need to get as far away as we can."

I took her into the forest once again. Far away from Kai and the beasts and anyone else. It was the only plan I had.

When darkness fell, we hid in a thick tangle of juniper bushes. Alva had been strong and brave for so long, but there in the thicket, she cried tears of pain.

"Where are we going?" she asked.

"To Dad," I said without thinking, but it made sense as soon as I said it. We were going to Dad. He was out there on Fair Isle in the North Sea, last time we spoke, and if we could only get to him, then we wouldn't be alone anymore. And then suddenly I remembered what our neighbor had said about boats that time in the kitchen.

"We're going to Djupevik to catch a boat out to Dad," I whispered, and Alva nodded and sniffed, safe in the belief that I had a plan.

I stood in the basement of the yellow house and studied the maps as Alva lay feverish and fast asleep in an unfamiliar bedroom. I studied the arrows on the maps more, the pattern formed by the drawing pins, the comments scrawled in felt-tip pen. They had written numbers in red, and in a few places, these had been scribbled out and new, higher numbers had been added. In other places were words like "rough," "crowded," "worth checking out."

One of the maps covered the area here, along the coast. There was a thumbtack by a place I understood must be the yellow house. A thick black line had been drawn from the house along the road leading to the coast, with a thinner green line through the forest, both leading to the same destination. *Djupevik*. It was circled in red pen. On the wall to the right was a nautical chart. It was circled in red there too.

I pulled out the tacks pinning the map to the wall and took it down. As I did so, a note that had been stuck in the gap between the two maps floated to the floor. There was a list written in pen, in old-fashioned, cursive handwriting: *raincoats, 2 woolly sweaters, spare woolly socks, 2 life jackets, 2 medium water bottles, trail mix, canned food, bread, insulin pens, needles, glucose meter, 2 waterproof gloves, 16-mm rope, wedding photos (don't forget waterproof bag!).*

I smiled. A real, proper smile, the kind that makes a sound of its own.

Whoever had lived in the yellow house had also traveled to Djupevik, I was certain. They'd planned a sea crossing. So it must be true: there were boats. A way out. My plan was a good one.

Alva slept deeply in the big bed. I smiled and rested my cheek against hers for a moment. Her skin was still clammy. I lay there for a short while; a stolen good night cuddle before I moved my head over onto my own pillow and fell asleep.

I dreamt of the sea. Of foamy swells and a boat that rocked, and of Dad.

# NINE.

**I picked some vegetables from the garden and fired up** the wood-burning stove. I fried the vegetables with a few eggs, then set the kitchen table. Alva shuffled into the kitchen in a pair of baggy gray wool socks she'd pulled up to her knees. Her cheeks were red and her eyes were glassy. She smiled when she caught sight of the food, though, and crossed her legs under her on the kitchen chair.

"I'm pretending this is our house," she said after a short while. "You're the dad and I'm the mom."

"Who's the baby?"

"Don't say that," Alva answered, piercing a carrot with her fork. "Teddy isn't here, you know that."

"Sorry." I passed her a glass of water and an aspirin. "Here, take this."

She swallowed the tablet without any complaints; in fact, she barely gagged at all. The old Alva would have demanded that Mom crush the tablet to a powder and mix it into some chocolate spread.

"I'm going to pretend that we'll be living here forever," Alva continued. "And one day we find some wild horses in the forest, and we tame them and let them live in our garage. I'll feed them carrots and look after them, and we can all go on big, long rides together."

"To Djupevik?"

"We don't need to go to Djupevik," Alva said firmly. "Daddy has his own horse, one that can swim, and they'll swim across the sea and find us."

After we'd eaten, we found some drawing things in a desk in the living room and Alva spread everything out on the living room floor, covering the space in colored pencils and sheets of paper. I brought one of the maps up from the basement and sat on the sofa with it. I studied it carefully, doing my best to memorize the routes that had been marked up between here and Djupevik. There was a third option too, I noticed; a longer route to the north, going around the forest. I borrowed one of Alva's pencils and added it to the map just in case.

"What color do you want your horse to be?" Alva asked. "Mine's going to be white with black spots, like Pippi Longstocking's horse."

"I'd like a brown horse, please," I said. She nodded in acknowledgment and picked up the brown pencil.

Alva's fever disappeared that day. We ate canned spaghetti for dinner, and while I relaxed on the sofa and read some old Donald Duck comics, Alva searched the house for treasure. I helped her move the books and lamp on the bedside table to make room for all the treasure she found: a recipe book dedicated to desserts, a scarf with white birds on it, a velvet-covered box filled with cutlery, and a tablecloth hand-embroidered with Christmas trees. Alva had also found a gold necklace hidden under a pile of ladies' underwear in the chest of drawers. She insisted on wearing it.

"It's the most beautiful thing I've ever seen in my *whole* life!" she said dramatically, then started licking the tiny white gemstones.

"Eugh, what are you doing?"

"It's what you do to see if it's *real* or not," she answered, rolling her eyes at me.

"And did it pass the test?"

"One thousand and seven percent *yes*!"

I smiled and handed her another aspirin tablet before tucking the duvet in tight around her.

"Abdi," she murmured.

I had just turned out the light and was closing the door behind me.

"Yes?"

"I need Teddy."

"You've managed OK up till now without him."

"But now I'm in my house, I need him."

"We left him behind to look after the old house," I sighed. "But I'll see what I can find."

After searching the entire house, I eventually found an old doll in one of the plastic boxes in the basement. The doll's eyes had once been able to open and close, but now one eye was sealed shut while the other was stuck wide open, leaving her with a permanent wink. She barely had any hair left, just a few rough, straggly yellow strands, and her dress was missing some buttons.

"She's a bit funny looking," I mumbled as I came back into Alva's room. "But it's the best I can do."

"Poor thing!" Alva exclaimed, pulling the doll into a close embrace. "She's been living out in the forest, just like us, but she doesn't even have a big brother to look after her. She was all alone!" Alva stroked the doll's remaining tufts of hair.

"Look!" she went on, holding her up to show me. "Look how tired and scared she is! And her sad eyes! The beasts killed her mommy. I'm going to be her mommy now, aren't I, Abdi?"

I nodded. My sister murmured comforting words in the doll's ear and stroked her head.

"Everything's going to be OK now, we've found a new home," I heard her tell the doll. I shut the bedroom door behind me.

# TEN.

**We were safe in the yellow house for two days.**

I was in the garden pulling up carrots. The sky was blue and the sun was shining. I had removed my sweater and dropped it on the grass at my feet. A few bees were buzzing around the sunflowers in the garden bed. A magpie shrieked as it flew over my head. A second magpie replied from the top of a tree. That was when I heard footsteps on gravel.

I dropped the carrot I was holding and crossed the lawn in an instant. I slipped in through the French door and made my way to the bedroom, where Alva was sitting on the bed looking at pictures of various desserts in the recipe book she'd found. The doll was propped up beside her, one blue eye staring straight at me. I said nothing, but put my finger to my lips and nodded in the direction of the yard.

I held my breath.

"Hello? Anyone home?" a man's voice called from outside.

"People!" Alva said with relief. "It's people, Abdi, don't be scared."

"We don't know if they're nice people," I whispered back.

"They can help us!" Alva said. "Come on, let's go down and open the door. We can ask them!"

She shuffled across the bed and her feet hit the floor with a thud.

"No!"

"Abdi," Alva said in a comforting tone. "Abdi, it's all right!"

"No," I repeated, grabbing her arm firmly. "This is dangerous, don't you see? Don't you remember what happened with Mom? And Kai? Not everyone is nice. We can only trust each other now."

At that moment I heard a window smashing, followed by thuds and the tinkling of glass, then a click, the turning of a lock. The front door was pushed open with a bang. Heavy footsteps. Men's voices.

We didn't move an inch.

Alva looked at me in terror. She expected me to do something; to have a plan. But I couldn't move, couldn't think.

The men's footsteps trailed off into the living room. We heard them talking in there and then they were back in the hallway, outside our bedroom door. Someone grabbed the handle and the door swung open.

There were two men, one tall and broad wearing an orange cap and a rifle green jacket. The other was a little smaller, but he looked fit, as if he ran marathons and went to the gym back when the world was normal. He was wearing a turquoise hooded jacket and a pair of sunglasses that he'd pushed up onto his head. He smiled when he saw us, but his smile didn't reach his eyes. They were narrowed and cold.

"It's polite to open the door when people knock, don't you think?" he asked, looking at me.

"We didn't know if you were nice or not," Alva said.

"Oh, we're nice," he sneered.

His friend said nothing, but he was the one who scared me most. He loomed in the doorway, his eyes sweeping over the shelves and cupboards in the room.

"Are you going to help us?" Alva asked.

"What do you need help with, little one?" The smaller man flashed his sly grin once again. He took another step into the room and picked up a sheet of paper on the bed.

Alva had drawn a yellow house in a forest with two figures standing beside it, smiling. It wasn't difficult to work out that they were supposed to be us. The man let out a snort and chuckled.

"Very sweet," he said, dropping the picture.

The bigger man's gaze suddenly rested on me.

"Where's the food?"

"We've eaten it all," Alva replied. Both men guffawed coarsely, but I didn't know if they were laughing at Alva or at me, standing there in silence, allowing a five-year-old to respond on my behalf.

"Enough of the nonsense," the smaller man barked. He'd stopped laughing.

The man nodded to his friend. "Let's search the house. The guy who lived here used to salt his own mutton. There must be some other treats for the taking too."

They disappeared in search of the kitchen. We heard them fumbling about, slamming cupboard doors, pulling things off shelves and throwing them onto the floor. One of them swore and said something about crackers.

"Abdi," Alva said carefully, taking my hand. "Abdi, we have to do something. They're taking our food, Abdi."

I don't know if it was the sound of my name or the feeling of her hand in mine, but something woke me with a jolt. I jumped: I could move again, talk again. Make a plan.

I pulled a few thick sweaters out of the wardrobe and helped Alva to put one on, followed by a pair of pants and some socks. I stuffed the packet of aspirin in my back pocket.

One of the men had gone to the basement. I could hear him rummaging around down there. The other man was in the living room. Something smashed against the hard floor, then I heard a triumphant cry.

"Score!"

"What is it?" the man in the basement grunted. It must have been the bigger of the two who was downstairs.

"Whiskey, man!" the man in the living room shouted. "The good stuff!"

We slipped out into the hallway. Alva went first, tiptoeing exaggeratedly like some sort of thief in a cartoon. The bag was still in the hallway, all packed and ready to go. The men hadn't spotted it. I pulled on my shoes and Alva managed to get hers on all by herself. Fast, silent movements. We were barely breathing.

"Anything good down there? Any meat?" the man in the living room shouted. We heard a snort from the basement. "Have those damned kids really eaten everything?"

More rummaging in the basement, but no response.

"*Did you hear me?* Any meat down there?" the man shouted from the living room. A cupboard door was slammed closed.

Was he on his way here?

I grabbed the backpack, Alva opened the door, and we ran. As fast and as silently as we could. Over the gravel, behind the garage, into the trees.

It felt wrong running away from people—from a warm house with food—and into a forest where beasts hunted us. But something bad was bound to happen if we stayed, I could feel it in my bones.

# ELEVEN.

**"What are we going to do, Abdi?" Alva asked. She was** sitting with her back against a tree trunk. She wasn't complaining, and there were no tears in her eyes as she asked the question. She simply wanted to know the plan.

"We can wait here, then go back to the house in the morning and see if they've moved on."

"I wish I was good at climbing trees. Then I could climb to the very top and hide. It's scary waiting here."

"I'll make us a den to hide in. Want to give me a hand?"

"Yes," Alva replied, sounding determined. I asked her to fetch twigs and branches, but not so far into the forest that she couldn't see me anymore. Alva carefully placed the doll against the tree and managed to gather a little pile of sticks before losing interest.

"I want to do something else," she sighed.

"Do you want to sort something out for us to eat?"

She inhaled slowly, then exhaled with a snort: "*OOOOOOK*."

"I'm busy making the den, so you'll need to deal with it yourself," I said, passing her the bag.

Having some responsibility seemed to give her a boost. Alva rummaged around and took charge, grunting with effort and humming every so often. I had just finished up our den when she announced that our food was ready. She'd arranged two bark plates on a tree stump and dragged two large stones over for us to sit on.

"How on earth did you manage to move those stones?" I asked, genuinely impressed.

"With my big muscles," she said, flashing me a grin.

Between the bark plates Alva had placed a can of ham, a can opener, and two apples. The lid of the can was covered in dents and scratches.

"I couldn't get it open," she added, sounding disappointed as she passed me the can opener.

"I'll show you," I said, opening it slowly as she peered over my shoulder.

After we'd eaten, we crawled into our little shelter made of fir tree branches. The entrance was so small that only a child would be able to get inside, and from a distance it just looked like a pile of greenery. We curled up close with the big wool blanket from the backpack wrapped around us. The doll lay in the crook of Alva's arm, keeping watch with its one beady eye.

"Was I a good helper?" Alva whispered.

"So good," I replied, squeezing her tight.

I woke to the sound of footsteps. At first, I thought it was the men out walking. Maybe they'd finished ransacking the house and decided to make their way back where they'd come from. Maybe they were looking for us.

But then, I heard the unmistakable click of hooves on stone.

I placed a hand over Alva's mouth and she woke in an instant. The sounds were coming from the other side of the cluster of trees. From the slope behind the garage. The clicking was faint and getting fainter as the hooves crossed rocky terrain. It was as if the beast was creeping around. *Click. Click.* Then the sound over the gravel.

I couldn't ignore it; I had to see. I motioned to Alva to stay where she was and wriggled out of our den as quietly as I could. I hid behind a bush and glanced around me, but the forest was empty. I ran from one tree to the next, making sure each time there was somewhere to hide in case there were several of them, until finally I was close enough to be able to see the yellow house.

A tall, slim figure was on the front steps. Its coat was short and sleek. Its legs were long and curved back, like horses' legs. And its head was narrow and slightly flat, with small ears flush against it. Its neck was crooked, and its face leaned in close to the broken windowpane.

It stood there and peered into the hallway. Waiting for something.

And that's when I saw it—the scariest thing I've ever seen in my life.

The beast knocked.

Took a step back.

Concealed itself in the shadow of the porch.

The voices from inside the house were angry. I couldn't hear what they were saying; I could only make out shouting, followed by a thud, and then the door flew open so fast that the remaining glass panes clattered. The bigger of the two men emerged.

"Get lost!" he shouted.

The beast stepped out of the shadow, and with a groan, the man slumped forward as the beast disappeared past him into the house.

I ran.

# TWELVE.

**Alva was waiting outside our hiding place, but there was** no time to be mad. Without a word we stuffed our things into the backpack and started running.

We didn't dare use the flashlight, and we did our best to be as quiet as we could.

We ran until our muscles ached and our chests throbbed.

We ran until the sky grew light and the morning mist hovered white and delicate just above the earth.

Finally we crept under a large bush, wrapped the blanket around us, and fell asleep. We were so tired that sleep snatched us the moment we stopped moving, but fear followed me into my dreams and painted them red.

Alva was staring at me when I woke up. Her face was just a few inches from mine, her breath warm against my cheek.

"We should go to Djupevik and take the boat that goes to Daddy," she said. "I've made up my mind." She looked so serious that I couldn't help but smile.

"You're right, we should."

"Do you know the way?"

"By heart," I answered, pulling her in for a cuddle. "I've got the map from the yellow house too. And we've got food, and a knife, a rope, and some warm clothing. Our backpack is full." I felt proud.

"Please don't squeeze me so hard, OK?" Alva said, pulling away from me. "I'm not a baby."

We each had a cracker for breakfast. On the slope by the juniper bushes was a patch of bilberries, but they were all wrinkled and overripe. Alva still picked a handful and arranged them on top of a cracker.

"For you," she said, passing it to me. "Ta-da!"

"Thank you," I smiled, accepting it from her, and as I ate, she picked berries for her own cracker.

We found a path that led us further into the forest and followed it for a while. It had been a long time since anyone walked here. The branches had grown low, and I had to crouch down at various points. But that also meant no tall, menacing beasts or grown adults had passed through here in some time. Alva chatted away to the doll as we walked, but I didn't hush her.

Eventually the track led us out of the forest, and we found ourselves standing at the top of a hill with a view of fields and scattered farms and a tarmac road that snaked down the hillside, and, to the west, the glittering sea. The sun was high and the sky was pale blue, not a cloud in sight.

"It's that way," I said, pointing northwest. "Djupevik. That's the North Sea beyond it, and Fair Isle is beyond that."

Alva held the doll up so she could see too.

The quickest route would be to follow the road down, but I didn't dare take the risk. It was so open anyone would be able to see us for miles. Instead we followed the fences and hedges, always staying close to something we could hide behind. The farms we passed all looked abandoned. The windows were dark, and a few were smashed. I wondered what'd happened to whoever had been living there. Had they fled? Were they dead?

"I don't want to live in any of these houses," Alva said. "They're scary."

"Agreed," I said.

Silently we crossed the farmyard between a barn and a white farmhouse. A car had been abandoned by the barn ramp with all four doors left wide open, and the front door of the farmhouse had a big, gaping hole in it; someone had hacked their way through it with an ax.

Alva grasped my hand tight and we started running again.

"Maybe we ought to head into the forest?" I suggested, breathless, after a little while. Alva nodded and we followed a fence to the end of the field and climbed over it and into the trees.

"But not too far in," I added, "we mustn't lose our way."

The woodland terrain was tougher to cross. Trees and bushes formed a dense layer, scratching our faces and hands as we pushed our way through.

"We're making too much noise," Alva said. Branches and boughs crunched and creaked around her.

*Tick, tick.*

A twig snapped.

But we were standing still now.

Someone was coming!

Alva gasped and looked at me for a moment. Should we hide, or should we run?

We ran. Charged ahead. The forest was too dense for us to run in silence. We sprinted as fast as our legs could carry us. We heard steps behind us, the snapping of twigs, shrubbery thrust aside. Someone was coming and they were moving fast.

My backpack got caught on a branch. I left it dangling behind me.

Alva dropped her doll. She left it where it fell.

We ran.

And then the forest came to an abrupt end, and before us was a vast, roaring river. The current was moving fast, and further down the river, sharp rocks jutted out of the water. If we didn't drown, the current would catch us and cast us to our deaths against the rocks all the same.

Behind us we heard the beast approaching.

How was I supposed to choose?

"Abdi?" Alva squeezed my hand. "Abdi, hurry!"

I nodded and swallowed the lump in my throat, the two of us stepping out into the water.

The current took hold of us instantly, its strong hands grabbing at our legs and tipping us upside down. I grasped at Alva but could only get hold of one of her arms. Her body was pulled away from me, and she struggled to keep her head above water. Alva couldn't swim. What on earth had I been thinking? Were we mad? The blue-green water washed over me, thundering against my arm and trying to steal Alva from me. At the same time, the water pulled me down the rapids and the sharp rocks protruded upward, towering in the middle of the river's path, dark and menacing. Alva's head was underwater for a moment, then she appeared back at the surface, coughing and spluttering and spitting out water. I had to swim. I *had* to get us both back on dry land.

Then I caught sight of him. On the riverbank. He was at least six feet tall, covered in a sleek, dense coat. His legs were slim, his arms long, those coiled claws at the ends. An evil face and black eyes were staring right at us.

# THIRTEEN.

***We're going to die*, I thought to myself. The water sloshed** over me again and again. I flailed one arm around and kept Alva clutched tight with the other. The river seemed determined to drag me down. I tried kicking my legs, but the current was stronger, and I couldn't let go of Alva. I locked eyes with her above the froth for a fleeting moment, then her head went underwater once again. All the while, the beast simply stood there on the riverbank, watching us. He didn't move a muscle. He made no attempt to catch us.

Did Mom know she was going to die when she grabbed the kitchen knife and made her way out into the garden to face the beasts? When she shouted to me that I should take Alva and run?

I knew that I was going to die as I thrashed around in the rushing water. I knew that Alva was going to die.

But I was wrong.

Out of the blue, I spotted a broom handle in front of my face. Out of the blue, I heard someone shouting. I could only just hear whoever it was above the roaring of the river.

"Grab hold!"

I grabbed hold.

I clutched the broom handle with all my might. I allowed myself to be hauled up onto dry land with Alva in tow. Her head was still underwater, but I didn't have the strength to lift her up. Little by little we were pulled toward the opposite riverbank.

What was the beast doing?

I could no longer see him. Either he had vanished back into the forest, or he was in the river now, making straight for us.

Hands grabbed my shoulders and pulled me up.

"Alva," I panted, coughing up water.

"I've got her," the voice said, and then I spotted my sister beside me on the riverbank. Her face was bluish white. Someone was hunched over her, strong hands pumping her chest, a head leaning over her face and blowing air into her mouth.

"Alva," I panted again, and then it was as if I lost track of time, because one minute I was there on the bank of the river then I blinked and opened my eyes again to find that I was in a wheelbarrow, Alva sprawled halfway across my chest, staring at me with great intensity.

"He's awake," she said to someone.

"We're almost there," the voice replied.

"Where are we going?" I whispered to Alva. "What's going on? This isn't safe! You need to run, Alva. Run!"

But Alva simply shook her head and lay back down on my chest. I hugged her tight, unable to do anything.

The wheelbarrow stopped after a short while, and I heard a groan as someone let go of the handles. I heard footsteps and the creak of a door.

"You think you can manage the last few steps yourselves? I'm not sure my back can carry you any further."

I sat up in the wheelbarrow and looked around me. An older woman was standing on the threshold of a small cabin. She was wearing rubber boots and a green raincoat that was a few sizes too big, and a warm, inviting light streamed from the open door behind her.

"Can you manage?" she asked me again. I nodded, even though I wasn't certain. Alva was already on her way out of the wheelbarrow. She casually approached the woman and made her way past her, straight into the cabin, as if she'd been there many times before. I followed and found myself in a small mudroom where big winter coats were hanging on hooks and boots and work shoes lined the wall. I carried on into the living room. In the middle was a large wooden table with a bench on each side. A fire was burning in the stove, and in front of it were two thread-bare armchairs, each with its own footstool. The woman disappeared into another room and returned with a pile of dry clothing for us.

"Sit by the fire," she said, "and get yourselves out of those wet things before you catch your death."

We changed in front of the fire and each crept into an armchair. The woman fetched two wool blankets and placed one over each of us, and we were each handed a cup of tea. The tea even had honey in it. I drank mine greedily and savored the warmth that spread through my chest and stomach.

"My name is Lucy," the woman said, sitting on the footstool by Alva's chair.

"Like Saint Lucy?" Alva asked, wide-eyed.

"Just Lucy," she replied, smiling.

"We're Alva and Abdi," Alva said. "I'm five and a half and he's thirteen, and we're all by ourselves. I lost my dolly, and Abdi lost our backpack with all our food in it. We were drowning when you found us."

"Thank you for saving us," I said quietly, and the words felt far too small to describe what had happened.

"It was nothing," Lucy replied.

"Weren't you scared? Of the monster?" Alva asked.

"I could hardly stand by and watch you both drown, could I?" Lucy answered, getting back on her feet. I noticed that her hands were red, as if the outermost layer of skin had been peeled away. She had similar marks on her throat and her ear. They looked like burns.

She had her back to us as she pottered around by the kitchen counter.

I finished my cup of tea and stood up.

"Come on," I whispered, and flashed Alva a look. She shook her head.

"Thanks for the tea and everything, but we have to go now," I said firmly, taking Alva by the hand. She pulled away from me.

"Come on, Alva!" I hissed, trying to grab her by the arm. She slumped onto the floor, just out of arm's reach. I tried to catch her eyes again, but she wouldn't even glance in my direction. Instead, she crawled under the table.

"You can't leave now!" Lucy said, turning toward me. "It'll be dark before too long, and it's not safe out there. It's not up for discussion. You're both staying here."

"You're not in charge of us," I replied, and I felt fear tighten its grip on me. My entire body was tense; I was shaking. "Alva," I said, pressing on.

If I had to drag her out of here with my own two hands, I'd do it. But Alva had curled up into a ball and could no longer see me or hear a word I was saying.

"Listen," Lucy said, "there's no reason for you to leave now. You're just children. I'm not going to hurt you." She seemed resigned, but not angry. Her expression was kind.

"Thanks, but no."

"Well, what about some dinner? Wouldn't that be nice?"

"I'm hungry!" Alva shouted from under the table.

"If you still want to leave after that, then I won't stand in your way. Let's just have a little bit of food first. OK?" Lucy looked at me.

I was hungry. So hungry.

I shrugged. Gazed at the floor.

Lucy took this as a yes and turned back to the kitchen counter. She took some potatoes, carrots, onions, and turnips. Peeled and chopped them. Tipped them into a pan with some green lentils and a few pinches of various herbs and spices. She hummed as she cooked. I watched her every move. I perched myself on the arm of the chair, even though it was a little uncomfortable, and observed everything she did. Where she put the knife, what she put in the pan, the way she smiled at Alva. I couldn't relax for a single second.

A relentless stream of words poured out from under the table as Lucy cooked. Alva told her things that I'd long forgotten—the kind of food we used to eat at home, the time we'd been on vacation and stayed in a hotel, that night we'd spent camping in a tent in the garden, all about Christmas presents and board games and Dad's origami creations, the time we'd been swimming and Mom had cut her foot on a glass bottle someone had thrown in the water. There was no end to her chatter, and the more she told Lucy, the sadder I felt. It felt like I was filling to the brim with tears, and I could hardly bear it.

"Alva, stop!" I said more than once, but she didn't quit talking until Lucy placed the food on the table. She was quick to hop up onto one of the benches, and Lucy had barely managed to say "dig in" before Alva started devouring the meal in front of her. I shuffled over to the table and politely and emphatically thanked Lucy for the meal.

"It's very kind of you to share with us."

"It's very kind of you both to keep me company," she answered with a small smile. "It's just me here, so it's nice to have you two to liven things up a little."

"We're a lively pair!" Alva said with her mouth full. "That's what Mom always says. And noisy, too."

"I can believe it," Lucy chuckled.

The food was tasty, and it was warm. The woodstove sent waves of heat out into the room, making me sleepy and docile. I so wanted to collapse into the armchair in front of the stove. There wasn't a single part of me that wanted to go back out into the cold, dark evening.

Alva shimmied up next to me on the bench and rested her head on my arm. She'd eaten a large portion and she was so sleepy that she nodded off right there; she slumped further and further down until her head was on my lap, one hand gripping my leg tight, as if she were afraid that I'd leave her. I had to wake her up before it was too late. We needed to go.

Lucy was sitting across from me at the table, staring directly at me.

"Do you want to stay the night?" she asked. "It's up to you. But you're both very welcome to stay here, if you'd like."

I thought it over for a moment before I nodded.

That night Alva and I slept in the daybed, tucked up together. As tired as I was, I still didn't sleep much because it was impossible to turn off my brain. Alva talked in her sleep, whimpering occasionally like a little puppy. Lucy snored in the room next door. When the fire started to die out, I got up and placed a few more logs on it, checking at the same time that the wood beam she had secured across the front door was firmly in place. I carefully pulled the curtain aside and stared out into the dark night. Where had the beast who had been hunting us gone? Had he seen Lucy save us? Had he followed us here?

I crept back into the bed beside Alva and pulled the covers up to my chin. I had given up in the river. Just before Lucy's broom handle appeared, I had given up. I had been ready to let go of Alva, let go of everything, let the water simply take me. And part of me had felt a sense of relief in that moment. Relief at letting go of living any longer.

# FOURTEEN.

**I must have nodded off eventually, because suddenly** the room was bright, and both Alva and Lucy were standing at the kitchen counter.

"Abdi, Abdi," Alva sang, jumping across the kitchen to greet me. "You can't sleep all day, you know!" she said, poking my nose just like Mom used to do when I wouldn't get up. I couldn't help but smile, in spite of the sadness I felt in my bones.

"We're making breakfast," Alva went on, hopping back over to Lucy, who handed her three plates and directed her to set the table.

"Chickens are God's gift to hungry people," Lucy said, placing a frying pan with three fried eggs in it on the table. "And we've got tea too, but it's a bit weak. Tea bags are hard to come by these days."

I wrapped the woolly blanket around me and shuffled onto the bench beside Alva. She'd already started tucking in.

"This is the best thing I've eaten in my whole life!" she announced contentedly.

"You said that about dinner last night too." Lucy smiled. "You're very easy to please!"

"I just looove food!" Alva said, throwing her arms out emphatically.

"Calm down, Alva," I mumbled.

"I don't *want* to calm down!" she exclaimed. "I'm allowed to say what I think! I'm smart, actually, that's what Mom says. And clever too!"

Lucy chuckled into her mug.

As she ate, Alva enthusiastically regaled us with tales from her time at kindergarten, about the time she'd led the Saint Lucy's Day parade with a crown of candles on her head, and then about the pet rabbits Mom had promised her, but now she wasn't sure if she wanted rabbits after all because it was smart to have chickens. Maybe she wanted chickens instead.

"Can you stop talking?" I burst out irritably. If she didn't stop soon, I'd start crying, and I didn't want to cry, not in front of Lucy at any rate. "Mom's dead and everyone at kindergarten is probably dead too, and all the rabbits are dead, and nobody is going to give you any chickens. Don't you get it? Don't you understand *anything* that's going on? Don't you?" I hissed.

Alva looked at me. Her eyes were shiny, but she didn't shed a tear.

"I know Mom is dead," she said quietly. "I saw."

"Then stop acting like such a brat!" I shouted, getting up from the table and walking out on them. I hadn't even eaten my egg.

I leaned against the back of the house with my knees up in front of me and I cried, long and hard.

Perhaps I had expected Lucy to come looking for me. That was what grown-ups did; they offered comfort and told us off when we deserved it. But it was Alva who appeared around the corner of the cabin after a short while. She held back for a moment, watching me before cautiously approaching and crouching down beside me.

"Are you sad?" she asked.

I nodded. The tears were still running down my cheeks, and it was impossible for me to stop them.

"I'm sorry for being a brat."

"You're not."

"Not even a little bit?" she asked meekly.

"Not at all. I was just angry."

"Why are you sad?"

I let out a deep exhale and wiped my face with my sleeve.

"Just . . . everything."

"Lucy said it's normal to feel sad when you almost die, like we did," Alva told me in a somber tone. "But I'm not sad. Just happy I didn't die. And that *you* didn't die. And that we have something to eat. And that we met Lucy. And that the monster didn't catch us. Is it bad that I'm not sad? Is that why you're so cross?"

I shook my head and put my arm around her. Her body felt so delicate and fragile. It was easy, with everything going on, to forget how small she really was. And she was my responsibility: mine and mine alone.

The tears started running down my face again and my breath seemed to get stuck in my chest. I sobbed and sobbed.

"Abdi?" she said, worried. She stood up. She took my hands and led me back into the cabin, over to the armchair, all while I continued to weep.

"It's healthy to have a good cry," Lucy said kindly, sitting in the other armchair. "Nice and cleansing on the inside." She lifted Alva onto her lap and placed her red hands around her waist. Alva rested her head against Lucy's chest. I was a bit envious. It had been so long since anyone had looked after me; hugged me.

Besides Alva, of course. I had Alva.

"I'm sorry, Alva," I said, sniffing.

"It's OK, Abdi. I don't want you to be sad."

"There's no harm in feeling sad," Lucy said. "The way the world is now, it'd be strange if you weren't sad if you ask me."

"It's all just so hard," I mumbled.

"Too hard." Lucy nodded.

"Are you sad, Lucy?" Alva asked with concern.

"I am, all the time," Lucy said. "But still, I try to keep going."

"Mom was killed by a beast." The words felt heavy in my mouth, like cold, smooth, slippery stones.

"Abdi is looking after me now," Alva said.

"I can see that," Lucy answered, smiling at me.

"Do you know any dead people?" Alva asked.

Lucy nodded silently.

"What happened to your hands?" Alva asked. "Did the monster get you?"

"We need some more wood for the fire," Lucy said abruptly, then picked Alva off her lap, got up, and left the room.

"Abdi?" Alva said. "Is she mad at me? Should I go and say sorry?"

"It's OK," I said, smiling. "I'll sort it out."

I found Lucy in the woodshed, but I didn't mention our conversation by the fire. Instead, I offered to help her. Lucy showed me how to split the wood with an ax, then how to stack the chopped wood. It was important not to stack the pieces too close together.

I worked for a long time, and the large pile of wood was slowly but surely chopped and stacked. My muscles ached, but my head felt blissfully empty. I left the ax standing in the chopping block and made my way around to the back when I was done. Yellow fields of grain and green grassland extended out from the cabin and across to farms in the distance. Nobody had harvested the grain this year. I pumped water from the well and splashed a few handfuls against my face.

Lucy and Alva had made bread dough, and now they were playing cards at the table. I joined them for a few rounds of Idiot before we rolled the dough to make flatbreads that we cooked in a pan. It was the first taste of fresh bread I'd had in a long time, and Lucy made garlic butter and fried potatoes to go with them. It tasted amazing. Afterward I brushed Alva's teeth with a little toothpaste on a cloth, then she was allowed to stand on the front doorstep and spit her toothpaste out onto the grass. She asked to have her glass of water refilled twice, then she spat and giggled and dribbled toothpaste all over her sweater. I took a sip myself and showed her how to gurgle the water, but when she tried it, she choked and spluttered until her eyes watered. That was the end of our teeth-brushing attempts.

Alva crept into the daybed, and I tucked her in. Both Lucy and I received a good night hug.

That night, Lucy set the water to boil for tea and added a small spoonful of honey to each cup. We drank our tea in our armchairs in front of the fire, and my whole body felt warm and tired in the best of ways.

"I didn't mean to be ungrateful yesterday," I said after a while. "Thank you so much for saving us from the river. And for all the food you've given us. And for letting us sleep here. It's been amazing. Thank you so much."

"Your thanks is more than enough for me," Lucy said. "What kind of person would I be if I refused to help you both?"

"Not everyone . . ." I began, but I couldn't finish. I sipped my tea instead, let it swish around inside my mouth for a while before swallowing. I could feel Lucy's eyes on me. Then, she nodded.

"I know," she said.

It was hard to carry on a conversation of this kind. I changed the subject.

"Do you have any family?"

"Yes, but it's just me now."

"Where are they?"

"Dead," she said.

"I'm so sorry," I mumbled.

She looked at me again, and it struck me that perhaps she wasn't as old as I'd first thought. Her eyes looked young. They were big and wide and a little scared.

"How old are you?"

Lucy laughed. "What makes you ask that all of a sudden?"

"I was just wondering."

"Old enough to have had three grandchildren." Then she added: "And two daughters, both of them married, so really, I had four grown-up children. A large, lovely family."

I said nothing, just waited until she was ready to go on.

"We were spending a long weekend in the capital," she continued eventually. "The whole family, on July 2nd."

I nodded slowly, and felt my entire body tense when I realized what she was telling me. The second of July was the day the beasts had attacked the largest cities.

"I don't know exactly what happened," she said. "I mean, not in any detail. It all turned so chaotic, so quickly. We were at a restaurant in the city center, then all of a sudden they were there, the beasts. We didn't have a word for them then; we'd never seen anything like them. They attacked everyone in sight, and we did our best to hide, but the restaurant caught fire. I think a table with candles on it fell onto some curtains, I'm still not sure. It was so hard to work out what was going on."

She shook her head slowly.

"I've always thought of myself as a practical person. Someone who would do the right thing, whatever was required in a crisis. But I wasn't. I panicked. My fear overwhelmed me."

She fell silent, clasped her cup tight.

"Lucy?" I said gently, after a short while had passed.

She took a deep breath.

"How did you survive?"

"I don't know. I was in the hospital when I came round, so I only know what they could tell me. I'd passed out from smoke inhalation, but the back door had been left open and my head had been close enough that I'd been able to breathe. I was lucky, that was what they said." She spoke the last words with disdain.

"What happened to the rest of your family?"

"I'd rather not talk about it, OK?" Lucy stood up and placed her wool blanket back in the basket and her cup in the sink. Then she paused for a moment outside the door leading to her bedroom.

"I promise you, I'm not a bad person, Abdi," she said. "You're both safe with me. And it means a lot to me that you're here." She closed the door quietly behind her, and I was left alone by the fire for a while, before I turned out the lamps and crept into the daybed beside Alva.

I slept well that night. Perhaps Lucy was right; perhaps my tears had cleansed me.

But my dreams were the same as how they always were. There was no escape for me there.

# FIFTEEN.

**"Will you come with us to Djupevik?" Alva asked as** we sat at the table eating breakfast. Lucy shook her head.

"Why not? We're going to an island where there aren't any monsters, and Daddy is there," Alva said. "Daddy's really nice."

"I'd rather stay here."

"But why? You have to come! It's better there! No monsters," Alva pushed.

"I can't leave this place," Lucy replied. "My father built this cabin with his own two hands, I used to come here as a little girl, and my girls would spend their summers here when they were little, and . . . this cabin is all I have left. But you two could always stay here with me, you know," she added swiftly. "There's room enough for the three of us. And I'll make sure you're well fed and safe. You don't need to go."

"We have to find Dad," I said. Lucy nodded and stood up. She started wiping the counter, moving quickly.

"Please, Lucy," Alva urged. "Come with us."

"Yes," I added. "It's not safe here. Come!"

Lucy turned and studied us both long and hard before letting out a sigh.

"I can't. You're probably right, Abdi, it's not safe here anymore. But if I'm going to die, I want to die here in my father's cabin."

She took a deep breath and went on: "But I'll come with you to Djupevik and see you off. You don't have to travel alone. We'll leave first thing tomorrow morning."

"You're so nice!" Alva shouted, running over to her and throwing her arms around her waist. "The nicest Saint Lucy that ever lived!"

"I'm just Lucy."

"Saint Lucy is here! Bringing good cheer!" Alva squeezed her tight.

Lucy laughed.

"All right then," she said, stroking Alva's head.

Lucy took us to an abandoned farm nearby. Alva was allowed to sit in the wheelbarrow on the way there, but she had to walk back because the wheelbarrow had been filled with potatoes, carrots, turnips, and broccoli.

"I'm not going to eat that broccoli, just so you know," Alva said resolutely.

"How on earth can you be picky at a time like this?" Lucy asked.

"I'm not picky, I just don't like broccoli!"

"That makes you picky," I said.

"It does not!" Alva roared, and her voice echoed across the fields. She stopped all of a sudden and covered her mouth.

"Sorry, I forgot," she whispered. I took her hand in mine and whispered back that it was OK, I didn't think anybody had heard.

It started raining as we took the vegetables inside. The water hammered down against the tin roof of the cabin, the wheelbarrow, us. We were wet through by the time we'd brought in the last load. Alva dropped the vegetables just inside the door and shook herself off enthusiastically.

"I'm a dog!" she cried, laughing, sending raindrops flying all around her.

"Into your bed, little doggy!" Lucy said, smiling. "Or we'll trip over you." Alva sank down onto all fours and crawled away. I placed the vegetables I was carrying down on the table and picked up the ones Alva had brought inside while Lucy started peeling potatoes with a sharp knife. We only ate breakfast and dinner—there wasn't enough food for any more meals than that—and now that dinner was approaching, we were all ravenous.

"What do you both say to a spot of fish?" Lucy asked. "What with it being your last evening here?"

"Is it sushi?" Alva asked, sounding apprehensive.

Lucy laughed.

"No, it's dried fish."

Alva mulled it over for a moment, weighing the hunger she felt against her suspicions about trying something new. Eventually, she agreed, so long as she wouldn't have to eat it all if she didn't like it.

"Could you fetch the fish from the shed, Abdi? It's hanging from the rafters." I nodded and pulled my boots on. I grabbed Lucy's raincoat; it was so long that it reached my knees.

The rain had created deep grooves in the ground outside, causing the water to run downhill toward the river. Shaggy-looking gray clouds rolled over the fields and the air carried a slightly pungent scent, like wet fur.

Wet fur?

I froze. Stopped dead in my tracks between the cabin and the shed. Warm yellow light flooded from the windows of the cabin, but elsewhere there was only rain and clouds to be seen. I looked intently all around me. Was there something moving over there to the left?

Had I imagined the smell? Could it have been a hare or a fox lurking nearby? A lone dog on the run?

I sniffed in deeply.

I could smell earth, chimney smoke, and . . . wet fur.

The hairs on the back of my neck stood up.

I took one cautious step back, then another.

I turned and ran. In through the door, slamming it closed behind me, barricading it with the beam left in the hallway. Lucy and Alva were already on their feet, on guard.

"I could smell wet fur," I said, breathless. "Outside, I couldn't see anything, but I'm sure there's something out there."

"Get changed, both of you, quickly!" Lucy commanded.

"Why?" Alva asked, but the look Lucy sent her was enough to get her moving without any more questions. We pulled off our wet clothes and grabbed the first decent things we could find in Lucy's wardrobe. Nothing fit, but everything was warm and dry. In the meantime, Lucy drew the curtains and extinguished the paraffin lamp on the table. Only the flames in the stove lit the room now. It had started to grow dark outside, and the heavy rain clouds gathered around the cabin.

"Abdi, move that chest of drawers," Lucy said. She kept watch by the window.

"Where?" I asked, bewildered.

"Just to the side, so you can get to the trapdoor behind it." I did as she asked, and sure enough, down by the baseboard behind the large red chest of drawers was a small trapdoor leading out into the darkness.

"What do I do with it?"

"If the beast gets in, take Alva out through that trapdoor and run," she said without looking at me.

"What about you?"

"I'll stay here and make sure he doesn't chase you."

There was no time to object; at that moment, the doorknob began rattling. It jumped up and down, shaking the entire door. When the handle failed to open, whoever was standing outside began kicking and pounding. But the beam we'd barred the door with was solid. There was no way anyone could kick it down.

Then there was a bang. Something had been thrown at the door with incredible force. The noise reverberated around the room, but everything held firm.

Silence fell.

We couldn't see what was happening outside. We stood in the middle of the room and all three of us held our breath. I could hear the sound of my own heart beating in my chest. Alva had positioned herself in between us and was clutching my hand tight in hers. Lucy stroked her cheek tenderly.

"Everything's all right, little one," she lied.

The attack on the door began again in earnest. The wood boomed. It creaked and splintered under the force.

We heard a wheezing snarl as the weapon was tugged free from the door.

The beast had found the ax I'd left in the chopping block.

Alva whimpered softly.

Lucy and I exchanged a glance above her head.

The beast hacked at the door again. And again.

The door was strong and solid and bolted tight, but I knew it would yield eventually. The inside had started to splinter. Sharp, fat shards of wood rained down on the floor below. With every swing of the ax, the gash grew larger.

The beast would soon be through.

Lucy crouched down next to Alva.

"Take care of Abdi," she said, kissing her cheek and drying Alva's tears with her sleeve. She stood up and pulled me into an embrace. Her body was warm and she smelled of woodsmoke and soap.

She looked me in the eyes and whispered, "I'm so glad I met you both."

Then she quickly pulled away, ushering us into the bedroom and closing the door behind us. I heard her dragging the dining table in front of the door, a thud as she flipped it over onto its side.

"We can't leave Lucy," Alva whined.

"We've got no choice," I said, wrapping a big black raincoat around her.

"This is just like what happened with Mom," Alva said tearfully. "She's going to die."

"Yes," I replied, because what else could I possibly say to her? We'd been through all of this before.

*Run,* Mom had shouted, and that's what we had done, but maybe we should have stayed behind to help her. If it had just been me here, I'd have stayed this time. Fought alongside Lucy, instead of sneaking away like some sort of coward. But Alva was standing beside me, small and scared inside the enormous raincoat, and if I didn't save her, I'd never forgive myself.

Then all would truly be lost.

"Come on," I said, creeping through the trapdoor, out into the cold, wet evening. Alva was right behind.

We sneaked along the side of the house. The grass was wet and muddy, and my pulse sang in my eardrums.

We heard thuds inside the house, and when I glanced around the corner, I saw that the front door was wide open. Lucy had opened the door to let the beast in.

She was shouting something, and her voice quivered with hatred and fury.

Suddenly everything was lit up brightly. The cabin was on fire. It burned fast and ferocious, and within seconds, the inside was filled with orange flames. The windowpanes shattered and the flames forced their way into the open air and up the outside walls.

We kept watch from a distance, but neither Lucy nor the beast emerged.

# SIXTEEN.

**We returned to the abandoned farm where we'd** harvested vegetables earlier that day. It was hard to leave. Lucy had sacrificed everything for us, but there was nothing we could do for her. Alva shuffled along behind me in silence, her arms hanging limp by her sides, her head bowed. The large raincoat hood covered her face entirely.

When we reached the farm, Alva refused to come inside the house. I found a hiding place for her between two shrubs and used a rock to break the glass pane in the front door.

I searched the house for anything we could use. I couldn't find a backpack, but beside a large desk in the living room was a leather satchel crammed with books, papers, and a laptop. I emptied the contents onto the floor and stashed two hats, a large scarf, and a flashlight I found in the hallway, as well as a knife from the kitchen knife block and a water bottle. The kitchen cupboards were empty. Lucy or someone else had already cleared them of any food.

The door into one of the bedrooms was open, and lying on the floor in the middle of the room was a brown teddy bear that seemed almost as if it had been waiting for us. I gave it a quick cuddle myself before running out into the farmyard and over to the shrubs where Alva was sitting.

"For you!" I said excitedly, passing her the bear.

"Ohh!" she sighed, clutching it to her chest in a tight embrace. "We'll save you, Teddy," she whispered to it, "but no shouting, OK?"

Alva, the bear, and I trekked for several hours, through the evening and into the darkness of the night. It felt more important now than ever that we make it to Djupevik. Eventually we had to rest, and I made a new den for us out of branches and leaves, where we managed to catch a few hours' sleep. The nights were starting to get colder, and we didn't have a wool blanket to wrap around us anymore. We pulled on our hats and cuddled close with one raincoat below us and the other on top. I wrapped the scarf around Alva. I was shivering with cold when I woke a few hours later and my fingers and toes were numb. Alva was sitting beside me, stroking the bear's head as she whispered words of comfort. We drank water from a stream and ate some wrinkled bilberries for breakfast.

We followed a track along the outskirts of the forest. We didn't speak. Neither of us had the energy. Neither of us had the energy for anything but placing one foot in front of the other and moving forward.

It grew warmer as the sun rose higher in the sky. The grass and heather were slow to dry out, and in several places, it was muddy and wet after the previous evening's downpour. I helped Alva over the dampest sections.

By afternoon we had reached the main road. There had once been heavy traffic going in both directions here, but now there wasn't a vehicle in sight. I tried to remember how long it had been since I'd last gone anywhere in a car—just an everyday thing, safe, with Mom and Dad and Alva. But the time before all of this was starting to feel hazy, like a dream.

"Come on," I said, leading Alva across the main road and onto a narrow, winding one. It passed crags and woodland, a pond with water lilies, deserted houses, and empty fields, getting closer and closer to the sea.

A utility pole had fallen in one place and was blocking our path; the cables dangled down onto the pavement like a straggly hammock to the next pole.

"Don't go anywhere near those wires," I warned Alva. "You never know." She nodded dutifully and took her time navigating over and around with the teddy bear tucked under one arm.

I hugged her when she reached the other side.

"You did well," I said. She nodded, but wouldn't look me in the eye.

"Do you want to hold my hand?" I asked. She shook her head.

"Alva, what is it? You haven't said a word all day."

Alva continued to stare at the ground, and I could see her hands clutching the teddy bear tight. Her knuckles were white.

"We're almost there," I said.

"OK," she whispered.

We followed the road uphill. Between the trees, we finally caught a glimpse of the sea. The wind was whipping the top of the water to a white froth, and the waves washed over a small landmass out at sea before pulling back again, over and over.

"Do you recognize that smell?" I asked. Alva shook her head and looked around her with concern.

"It's the sea," I said.

She said nothing.

"Not far now," I told her.

The road continued downhill toward a bridge, then further up to another winding slope, but between the bridge and the bay, like a shelf cut into the steep mountainside, was a narrow pathway. The pathway ended at a large wooden wharf at the bay's edge. There were about fifty people standing in a line that wound its way along the path. It was barely wide enough for one person, with rocky mountain on one side and a steep drop into the water on the other. The sea glittered, black as oil.

Everyone had come to Djupevik to escape by boat.

But there were no boats in the harbor.

# SEVENTEEN.

**The water stretched out ahead of us, endless and dark.** Djupevik was protected from the open sea by several rocks and small islands. The waves hit the small landmasses and the sea spray flew high into the air, foaming. A few seagulls circled above our heads, on the lookout for food.

I'd pictured an enormous ship waiting for us in Djupevik. A ship with cabins and cafés and a kind captain who'd welcome us onboard with the promise of taking us to safety.

I stared at the people standing in line along the pathway, trapped between the steep mountainside and the deep bay. What would they do if a beast jumped out from somewhere nearby? How could they possibly escape?

I sank down onto my haunches by the guardrail. I had to think.

Alva crouched down beside me.

"Is this the wrong place?" she asked after a while.

"No," I sighed. "I know that map like the back of my hand, and this is it. It's here. That's why everyone else is here too, to wait for the boat."

"What if the people aren't nice?" she whispered, flashing me a questioning look.

"It's a risk we have to take," I replied, and in that moment, I realized I'd made up my mind. There were no other options. We had nowhere to go, and no other way of reaching Dad.

Slowly we made our way downhill and over the bridge to the pathway. At the back of the line was a young man with long, unwashed hair and a beard. He deliberately moved, to make it clear that we weren't to go past him. There was no special treatment for children here.

When the darkness of evening fell, many people took food from their backpacks and bags and gathered in small groups to eat. We didn't have anything to eat, only the water in our bottle. I took a little sip and told Alva to drink the rest.

She was quiet, far too quiet. I felt her forehead but she didn't have a fever.

"Does your tummy hurt?" I asked. She shook her head slightly, took a little sip of water, then lay her head in my lap and closed her eyes. She was holding the teddy bear tightly. I wrapped the scarf around her and hoped she'd manage to get some sleep. I'd be keeping watch that night.

All the way along the path were sleeping people. Some had blankets and sleeping bags to stay warm, while others simply lay with their legs curled up to their chests. They were packed tightly together, and it would take no more than one sudden movement, a lurch in one person's sleep, to tip them over the edge. Falling asleep like this was only for those on the brink of exhaustion. What had they all been through before coming here?

I wasn't the only one keeping watch. A pair of men were standing on the wharf down below, and two women were sitting on the path with their legs dangling over the edge, both looking out to sea. I noticed a couple uphill too, and one on the hilltop not far away. I didn't know what their plan would be if the beasts came: there was no way for us to defend ourselves against them, and nowhere for us to run. But it made me feel a little better all the same, knowing I wasn't alone.

The hours drifted by, and it grew colder. The gusts of wind from the open sea swept over us and froze me to the bone. My whole body was shaking. But Alva was sleeping deeply in my lap, and I couldn't move without waking her. I thought about what lay ahead. There was nothing left for us here—nowhere to feel safe, nobody we could turn to for help, no food, no future. But out there, across the sea, a new place awaited us. A land free from danger, free from the beasts. And then there was Dad. I pictured him standing and waiting as the huge ship docked. The wind tousling his hair, his arms outstretched. Alva and I walking—no, *running*—along the wharf, throwing ourselves into his arms. And he would catch us both in his strong embrace, whisper that it was all over, all the awful stuff we'd been through, that we were safe. Even in this cold night, there was room for hope. I felt it in my gut, like a small, hot stone nestled away in the darkness. It would all soon be over.

I had almost fallen asleep. My head was heavy, my eyes blinked slowly.

That was when I heard it.

An engine, and a boat hitting the waves with rhythmic thuds.

Everyone else had heard it too. All of a sudden, the people sprang to life around us. Those who had been asleep woke with a start, and everyone stood up and started gathering their things. I woke Alva.

"It's time!" I cried, and I felt a smile spreading across my face. Our salvation had come.

# EIGHTEEN.

**An inflatable boat with an outboard motor pulled into** the harbor of Djupevik.

It wasn't a beautiful ship, and there was no kind captain waving at us from the prow. There wouldn't even be enough space for everyone onboard.

It was as if everyone who had been waiting had the same realization, at the same time, because all of a sudden they all started pushing, chasing the line further down the pathway as if that would secure their place. Some fell over, some shouted, others hushed them, warning that the beasts might hear them. Yet still people continued pushing. They wanted a spot on that boat, no matter how small and flimsy it might be.

A man at the very front was pushed with such force that he fell into the water. One of the men in the boat fished him out but didn't let him on. He was helped back on the wharf, then the man in the boat shouted something. I couldn't hear what he said, but some people further down the line started objecting.

"What did he say?" I asked the man in front of us. He turned around slowly and peered at me for a moment before replying.

"That there's only space for forty people."

"What? There's not space for forty people on that thing!" I exclaimed. Surely everyone could see that.

"Stay here, then," the man said. "Everyone else is saying he ought to take *more* people."

"Is there another boat waiting for us out at sea?" I asked. "A real ship?"

The man sneered.

"Are you going on vacation? Waiting for your cruise ship to swoop in and pick you up?"

None of this made any sense. We were going to be traveling such a long way. I'd studied the map carefully: the Shetland Islands were way out in the North Sea. There would be huge gusts of wind, and enormous waves to tackle. Such a small boat would never make it through.

I turned to the couple behind us in the line. A grown-up man with a protective arm around his wife.

"Is it true?" I asked imploringly. Someone had to tell me this was all a bad joke. That obviously there was a bigger ship waiting for us beyond the bay, that this was just the vessel that would be taking us there.

"I don't know," the man replied. "We just need to get away from here."

The men in the inflatable boat dumped a pile of orange life jackets onto the wharf, and the largest of them, a muscular man in a tracksuit, jumped out and started shouting instructions.

One by one, those who had been waiting took envelopes and valuables from their pockets, passing them to the man. Each of them was given a life jacket in return and allowed to clamber on. Once onboard they were packed in tight, like boxes in a moving van, seated all the way up to the edges. Some of them were practically on top of each other, and once they were in position, it was impossible for them to move. Little by little, the line moved down the path and the boat filled up. I looked around, at a loss. Nobody had told me we'd need to pay our way. We had nothing to give them. I felt a pang of relief. They wouldn't let us onboard without payment. We'd be left here on the pathway, and we could wait for the next boat: a bigger, better boat, with a captain who'd help us out without expecting anything in return.

A woman slipped on her way down the sloping pathway, and the man in front of her only just managed to reach out before she disappeared over the edge. It took two grown adults to haul her up and back onto the path.

She was shaking and crying. A man further back shouted at her and told them to hurry things up.

The boat was already full, but the man on the wharf continued directing people onboard. The woman who had fallen wept as she pulled on a life jacket and carefully climbed in. She ended up half-perched on the lap of a man who laughed and winked at his friend, but his friend didn't return the smile. The people in the boat looked pale and anxious. A few of them started complaining, saying that others ought to get off. "It's full, it's too full!" they repeated. The man on the wharf just shook his head before pointing at Alva and me. We were next.

"We've got no money," I said. "I didn't know."

He groaned loudly.

"What about valuables? Watches? Jewelry?"

I shook my head, but then Alva piped up beside me.

"We've got this," she called, coaxing the gold necklace she'd found in the yellow house out from under her sweater collar. The man leaned over and examined it for a moment before carefully unlatching it from around her neck.

"Take a life jacket and get onboard," he announced, standing back up again.

"We've changed our minds," I said softly. "We don't want to."

The man looked at me, and his expression was almost kind for a fleeting moment.

"You can't stay here, kid. You won't last long."

"But . . ." I began.

"Come on," he said. "You two are the last."

Those behind us in the line started yelling when he said that, but I could barely hear them. The fear inside me had jolted awake and was beating its big black wings with such speed and force that the rushing sound filled my eardrums. I couldn't hear anything above the noise.

"Abdi?" Alva said gently. "What is it?"

Her voice only just managed to break through the sound in my ears, and it took all my strength and courage to answer her.

"I don't think this is a good idea," I murmured. "Maybe we should stay here?"

"As a punishment?" Alva asked meekly.

"Punishment for what?"

"It was my fault. What happened to Lucy . . . I shouted."

The rushing in my ears stopped then. My fear curled back into itself. I didn't care about the people complaining around me, or the man in the tracksuit impatiently thrusting two life jackets forward in his hands, one for each of us. I crouched down in front of Alva.

"That wasn't your fault," I said firmly. "Not at all. None of this is our fault."

Alva nodded hesitantly.

"But what are we going to do?" I sighed. "I don't think the boat looks very safe, but there's no plan B. We could try to find another house around here, I don't know. What do you think?"

Alva nodded again, more resolute this time. Her expression was somber and thoughtful.

"Get a move on, come on!" the man urged, nudging us with the life jackets.

"Let's go and find Dad," she said. "Finding another house is no good. The monsters will find it too, in the end." She squeezed my hand and smiled softly. "I'll look after you, Abdi. It's going to be OK."

We took the orange life jackets, and I helped Alva do up her zipper. Someone with strong hands grabbed us after the man in the tracksuit lifted me and then Alva from the wharf and down into the small boat. There was almost no room for us inside. I perched on someone's knee, an elbow sticking into my back. Alva was placed in my lap. I managed to loop the strap of the leather satchel over my head and placed the satchel itself on Alva's knees. Alva stuffed the teddy bear's feet under the flap.

The outboard motor started up. The man in the tracksuit hopped into the back of the boat and the entire thing swayed from side to side.

"You've all got to stay calm. Absolutely no standing up. Is that understood?" the man shouted to everyone in the vessel. Some responded, but most just bowed their heads in acknowledgment. Alva leaned her head back on my shoulder and the sweaty, slightly peppery scent of her hair calmed me down. Kept my fear small and quiet.

We left Djupevik and ventured out between the rocks and islets, out into the open sea. That was where the waves seized the small boat. With a firm grip they threw us up and down: each jerk of the boat slammed our bodies with such force it felt as if our teeth were rattling around inside our heads, as if our necks and spines were being compressed and extended like steel springs. The sea spray flew into the boat and coated our faces and clothing. I had our hats in my pocket, but we were packed in so tight it was hard work even to slip a hand in and fish them out. I eventually got hold of the hats and pulled them down over our ears. We were fortunate to be wearing big raincoats. Those sitting closest to the edge were already wet through. A young woman beside us was sitting right on the edge of the vessel. She had wrapped a thin blue cord around her waist and attached it to a small plastic hook just inside the boat, but even so, each time the boat dropped over a swell in the water, she was lifted a few inches into the air. It looked as if she might tumble out. Her denim jacket was drenched, and she was shaking. I took off my hat and passed it to her.

"Here, take it," I shouted.

"Thank you," she said, smiling in disbelief. I smiled back at her.

I could still see Djupevik, the vast forests and reddish brown stretches of heather and grassland, the gray and white rocks, worn down to a rounded smoothness after enduring thousands of years of waves and wind.

But before long the detail had faded, and the coastline was just a blurred, green stroke on the horizon far, far away.

We were surrounded by gray sky and deep bluish black sea, and the frothing white crests that threw us around.

Suddenly a voice spoke. It crackled and spluttered, forcing its way along the electromagnetic waves in the air and into a black and orange radio in the pocket of a tracksuit. I couldn't make out what the voice was saying. It was crackling far too much for that, and the voices of those around me were too loud. Everyone had started talking over one another, filled with hope and excitement.

"Silence!" thundered the man in the tracksuit, holding the radio up above his head.

The crackling voice broke through. The voice asked for our position and announced that they were on their way.

I squeezed Alva tight.

"We'll be safe soon," I whispered. "I promise."

**INGVILD BJERKELAND** is an author of picture books and novels for children and young adults. Her novel *Beasts* was nominated for the Nordic Council Children and YA Prize and was also voted by over 10,000 schoolchildren for the highest booksellers' award in Norway. *Beasts* is her first novel translated into English.

**ROSIE HEDGER** was born in Scotland and completed her MA (Hons) in Scandinavian Studies at the University of Edinburgh, where she graduated with a distinction. Her translation accolades include the English PEN Translates Award and the shortlists for the Petrona Award for Best Scandinavian Crime Novel of the Year and Oxford-Weidenfeld Translation Prize.

## SOME NOTES ON THIS BOOK'S PRODUCTION

The cover was designed by John Gall and the jacket, case, and interiors by Maya Tatsukawa. The text was set by Westchester Publishing Services, in Danbury, CT, using ITC Legacy Serif Pro, a family designed by American Ronald Arnholm for Linotype in 1992. Arnhold was first inspired by the 15th-century roman type by Nicolas Jenson that he encountered in a type history class; his italics for the family were inspired by the 16th-century work of Claude Garamond. The display was set in Becker Gothics, designed by James Puckett for Dunwich Type Founders, which pays homage to the 19th-century American lettering master George Becker. The book was printed on FSC™-certified 65gsm TGY woodfree paper and bound in China.

Production supervisor: Freesia Blizard
Associate managing editor: Danielle Maldonado
Editor: Nick Thomas

LQ